P9-CFO-240

Donated in honor of

Mrs. Jacqueline Sullivan
and
Mrs. Pamela Thacker
by
Marissa Capineri
June 1996

B252 © APCo

OZZIE
ON HIS OWN

By Johanna Hurwitz

Johanna Hurwitz

OZZIE

ON HIS OWN

illustrated by
Eileen McKeating

Morrow Junior Books   New York

Text copyright © 1995 by Johanna Hurwitz
Illustrations copyright © 1995 by Eileen McKeating

All rights reserved. No part of this book may be reproduced or utilized in any form
or by any means, electronic or mechanical, including photocopying, recording,
or by any information storage and retrieval system, without permission in writing from the
Publisher. Inquiries should be addressed to William Morrow and Company, Inc.,
1350 Avenue of the Americas, New York, NY 10019.
Printed in the United States of America.
1   2   3   4   5   6   7   8   9   10

Library of Congress Cataloging-in-Publication Data
Hurwitz, Johanna.
Ozzie on his own/Johanna Hurwitz; illustrated by Eileen McKeating.
p.   cm.   Summary: When Ozzie's best friend, his niece Roz, goes away for the
summer, he makes some new friends, but then his father has a heart attack,
and he feels very much alone.
ISBN 0-688-13742-3
[1. Death—Fiction.   2. Fathers and sons—Fiction.   3. Family life—Fiction.]
I. McKeating, Eileen, ill.   II. Title.   PZ7. H95740z   1995   [Fic]—dc20
94-20111   CIP   AC   r94

To the members of my writing group, whose friendship, advice, humor, and support assure me that I am never alone.
And to the memory of Sylvia Cassedy

Contents

OZZIE
ON HIS OWN

1
Mayonnaise

Nobody had more energy, more enthusiasm, more hobbies, more corny jokes, or more freckles than Ozzie Sims. However, here it was the morning of July tenth, in the middle of school vacation, and Ozzie was sitting on the steps in front of his house doing absolutely nothing. No one seeing him would guess that he was an avid coin collector, regularly made up his own riddles, knew how to knit and crochet, and was developing into a first-rate cook. Not many eight-year-old boys knew how to make a pot of vegetable soup from scratch or how to mix up their own batch of chocolate-chip cookies.

With so many ways to occupy his time, it was

not often Ozzie found himself sitting around doing nothing.

Mrs. Menzer, who lived farther down Ozzie's street, walked by with her large white poodle, Samantha.

"All alone?" she called out to Ozzie. It was a silly thing to say, Ozzie thought. Anyone could see he was sitting there by himself.

Ozzie nodded his head.

"When is Roz coming back?" Mrs. Menzer asked him.

Roz was Ozzie's best and only friend, even though she was two years older than he was. She lived in the other half of his two-family house and her mother was Ozzie's half sister. This made Roz Ozzie's niece. It was a bit unusual for an eight-year-old boy to be an uncle, but everything about Ozzie was a bit unusual. At least that's what Roz always said about him.

"She'll be home in fifty-two days," said Ozzie. He'd been keeping count. In the last year he had gotten used to doing everything with her. Now, with Roz away, the summer seemed endless. Roz had already been gone for twelve days, and for some reason they had been the longest, most boring twelve days of Ozzie's life.

"She's a lucky girl," said Mrs. Menzer. "Imagine spending a whole summer in England. I've always wanted to go there myself."

Ozzie wondered what Roz was doing right now. It was about ten o'clock in the morning. That meant it was about three o'clock in the afternoon in London, where Roz and her parents were staying. Roz's mother had been awarded money to do research for her studies, so she was probably at some library or other taking notes. But Roz and her father could be doing anything. Maybe, if he was lucky, Ozzie thought, he'd get another postcard from Roz today. He'd already gotten one from her and one from her parents. That was more mail than he usually got in a whole month.

The front door opened and Ozzie's mother came out. Mrs. Sims was a nurse, and during the school year she worked part-time at St. Francis Hospital. She had taken a leave of absence over the summer so she would be home to keep an eye on Ozzie.

Seeing Mrs. Menzer, she greeted her neighbor. "Hello," she said. "How are you doing on this hot morning?"

"My ankles are beginning to swell," Mrs. Menzer said. "As soon as I get home, I'm going to rest my legs."

"I'll walk Samantha," offered Ozzie. He often took their neighbor's dog for a walk.

"She's already had her morning walk," explained Mrs. Menzer. "I was just about to take her home."

Ozzie was disappointed. Walking Samantha would have passed some time. It was amazing how slowly the time went now that he was on his own.

"Maybe Ozzie can take Samantha for her afternoon walk," suggested Mrs. Sims. "Something has come up," she said to her son.

"What is it?" asked Ozzie, perking up. Maybe his father had phoned to say he was coming home from work early. Ozzie always had a good time doing things with him.

"I need a jar of mayonnaise. I want you to walk up to the corner of Kinkade and Corn and buy it at the deli there."

"Okay," said Ozzie, feeling disappointed. "Anything else?"

His mother shook her head. "Here's a five-dollar bill. Be careful with it," she said as she handed it to Ozzie. "Don't lose the change."

Ozzie put the bill in a pocket in his shorts and

set out in the direction of the deli. Though most people liked paper money, Ozzie was a coin collector, so he thought paper money was boring. Now, if he had the five hundred pennies that the piece of paper in his pocket represented, that would have been something different. As he walked, he kept an eye on the ground. He never knew when he might find a penny or a nickel that someone had carelessly dropped. A penny that was heads-up was supposed to bring good luck. But Ozzie would never pass up a coin that was tails-up, either. For him it was especially good luck if he found something that he needed for his collection.

At the corner, two doors before the deli, was a bank. Ozzie stopped in front of the building. He had just gotten a great idea. If he went inside, he could get ten rolls of pennies in exchange for the five-dollar bill in his pocket. Nowadays, it was getting harder and harder for him to find pennies that he needed for his collection. But if he got ten rolls all at once, he could look at the pennies and check the dates and the locations where each of the coins had been minted. He could also look for wheat pennies. These were pennies that had two sheaves of wheat in the design on the back. If he was lucky, there would be two or three pennies out of the five hundred that he could use in his collection. The rest he would have for his errand.

With this thought in mind, Ozzie pushed open the door into the bank instead of going to the deli. The cool air-conditioning felt great as he stood on line waiting his turn. He could hardly reach the counter, but by standing on his toes and speaking in a loud voice, he was able to tell the clerk what he wanted.

"This is pretty heavy," said the clerk, counting out the ten rolls. "Can you manage with them?"

"Sure," said Ozzie.

He put five rolls of coins in each of the pockets of his shorts. The bulky weight pulled the shorts so that they almost slipped off of him.

Ozzie decided that he had better check out the pennies at once. If he paid for the mayonnaise with some of the pennies, he might be giving up coins that he particularly needed. He looked around for a good place to examine the coins. If he didn't need them, he would just roll them back up and exchange them for paper again at the bank. He thought his mother would prefer that to pennies.

Ozzie sat down at the curb and pulled one of the rolls out of his pocket. Each roll was a mystery until he opened it. Maybe he'd find a rare, hard-to

find penny. He never knew, and that's what made his hobby so interesting. Excitedly he opened the first roll onto his lap. He began checking the tiny dates. He was hoping to find a 1971 D or a 1969 S, as well as several others. There was nothing he needed among the first group of fifty pennies that he examined, so he carefully put them back into the roll. Then he put that roll on the ground beside him. If he put it in his pocket, he'd get confused about which ones he'd checked and which he hadn't.

The second roll and the third didn't yield any good coins, either. But then Ozzie got lucky. There were *two* pennies that he wanted in roll four. There was a zinc penny from 1943 *and* a wheat penny. He had hit the jackpot. He stood up to put the two good pennies inside his pocket and to pull out the fifth roll from his right side pocket. However, the weight of 250 pennies on the left side of his body was too much for the elastic in the waistband of his shorts. Ozzie's shorts slipped down to his knees.

Ozzie grabbed for his pants in a panic. He hoped no one had noticed him standing there with his pants falling off him like a little baby. As he grabbed his shorts, his foot accidentally kicked out at the penny rolls on the ground. Two of them began rolling, and one of them slipped off the curb and down onto the street below. It kept rolling, and before Ozzie could manage to get it, the roll fell through the sewer grate. He heard it land with a small splash in the dark waters below.

Ozzie tried to put his hand through the sewer hole. Little as his hand was, it couldn't fit through. It was a very small relief to Ozzie that he hadn't needed any of those pennies for his collection. He still had to explain the unexpected loss of fifty cents to his mother. He hoped she wouldn't get angry. Somehow he often got himself in trouble doing things he shouldn't. But he never did anything that he had been specifically forbidden to do.

So even though there were six rolls still unexamined, Ozzie decided he had better hurry home at once and tell his mother. It was an accident. Anyone could have an accident.

He put the three rolls that he had examined back into his right side pocket. Then, holding up his shorts as he walked, he started home. He probably looked strange holding up his pants, he realized. But he would look a whole lot worse if they fell off again.

"You did what?" asked Mrs. Sims when Ozzie got home.

"I kicked fifty cents down the sewer. I didn't mean to do it. They just slipped and rolled into the street. But I have all the rest of the money. And there's two cents that I need for my collection. I'll pay you back for those, and for the fifty cents, too."

Ozzie took all the rolls of coins out of his pockets and put them on the kitchen table. "Here's the rest of the money," he said to his mother.

"Why does it look so different from what I gave you?" asked Mrs. Sims, sounding annoyed. "I remember distinctly that I gave you a five-dollar bill."

"Well, I stopped in the bank and they gave me these penny rolls," he explained. "You didn't say I couldn't do that," he added quickly, defending himself.

"It never would have occurred to me," said Mrs. Sims. "Now I have another question," she said to her son. "What happened to the mayonnaise?"

"Oh." Suddenly Ozzie remembered the original purpose of his trip to the corner. "You mean the mayonnaise that you wanted me to buy at the deli?"

"Exactly. That's the very mayonnaise that I mean," said Mrs. Sims. But she wasn't scolding. She was laughing. "Ozzie, you're old enough to remember a jar of mayonnaise for fifteen minutes."

"Mayonnaise isn't very interesting," Ozzie confessed.

"Maybe not, but your lunch will taste rather dry without it. Do you think you could try again? Go up to the corner and buy me a jar. And perhaps you could stop at the bank and exchange some of these pennies into dollar bills."

"Okay." Ozzie sighed. It wasn't exactly an exciting way to spend the summer, buying or not buying mayonnaise. But at least it passed the time. He looked at the clock in the kitchen. It was almost noon. That meant, in London, Roz would soon be eating supper. After supper came bedtime. Soon it would be only fifty-one days until Roz came home again.

2
Mrs. Menzer's
Chicken Coop

Although the day had gotten off to a bad start, some incredibly wonderful things happened that afternoon. They began after Ozzie finished his lunch. He walked Mrs. Menzer's dog as he had promised to do.

However, instead of returning sedately to the front door of her home as she generally did, Samantha began to chase a squirrel. Ozzie, who was holding on to her leash, was pulled along, too. Samantha raced after the squirrel, toward Mrs. Menzer's backyard. Ozzie had never paid any attention to his neighbor's yard. In fact, he couldn't even remember if he had ever been in it before. So he was very surprised to notice a small wooden shack there.

After the squirrel had escaped to a tree and Samantha had accepted defeat, Ozzie took the dog around to the front again. He handed the leash over to her owner.

"What's that little house in your yard?" Ozzie asked Mrs. Menzer.

"You must mean my chicken coop," said Mrs. Menzer. "At least it was a chicken coop once upon a time. When my husband was alive, we used to have half a dozen hens and a rooster. Every morning he went out and picked up their eggs before breakfast. Then the town changed the zoning laws and said we couldn't keep livestock of any sort. So we gave the chickens to my brother, who lives out in the country, where they don't have any rules like that. The coop's been empty ever since."

Mrs. Menzer reached into the pocket of her dress and took out some coins, which she pressed into Ozzie's hand. "This is for you. Buy yourself an ice cream this afternoon," she told him.

"You shouldn't give me anything," said Ozzie. "I walk Samantha because I like to, not because I want to make money." Yet Ozzie could not help inspecting the dates on the change in his hand. He didn't need any of the coins for his collection.

"I know," said Mrs. Menzer. "But in this hot

weather, it's a wonderful thing for me to have you walking Samantha. So I'll feel better if you take it. Then I can ask you again tomorrow."

"I'll walk Samantha tomorrow and every day if you want me to," offered Ozzie. "Can I go look inside your chicken coop?" he asked Mrs. Menzer.

"That dirty old place? There's not much to see," Mrs. Menzer said, sounding surprised at Ozzie's request. "I've been meaning to have it pulled down for years. It's really an eyesore."

No one knew more chicken riddles or chicken jokes than Ozzie, but he had never been inside a chicken coop in his life. So he ran to the back of the house and pushed on the wooden door. The door was warped with age and didn't fit easily into its frame, but he managed to open it. Inside the coop, there was some old lumber stored in one corner and a couple of old chairs. There was a glass window, but it was so dirty that almost no light was able to come through. There was a damp, musty odor about the little house. Ozzie wondered if that was the smell of chickens or just dirt and age. Whatever it was, it didn't discourage Ozzie. In fact, he had a wonderful idea.

He ran back to the front of the house, where his neighbor was sitting on her porch. "Mrs. Menzer," he said eagerly, "would you let me make your chicken coop into a clubhouse? I could clean it out and fix it up. It would be perfect."

"A clubhouse? Out of the chicken coop?" asked the elderly woman doubtfully.

"It would be wonderful!" said Ozzie. "I'll clean it up and wash the window." He thought of what he could say to convince Mrs. Menzer. "I'd walk Samantha for you every day all summer. Then you could rest your feet in the hot weather."

"Well, I guess it would be all right," said Mrs. Menzer. "It does seem a shame that it's just standing there empty and is never used for anything."

Ozzie threw his arms around his neighbor and gave her a hug. "Wait till I write and tell Roz. She won't have her own clubhouse in England," he said excitedly.

"You could take out the wood and put it in my garage," suggested Mrs. Menzer. "And I have an old bridge table in my basement that you could use. There's no electricity or heat, but you won't need that in the middle of the summer."

"I'm going to tell my mother, but I'll be right back to start cleaning," said Ozzie. "Samantha, you can be the club mascot," he shouted over his shoulder to the dog as he ran off.

At that moment, the fifty-two remaining days of summer vacation seemed like very little time for all the things he wanted to do.

Mrs. Sims was in the midst of reorganizing the linen closet when Ozzie returned to his house. She looked up from a pile of towels.

"I need to take the broom and some old rags and the bottle of window cleaner," Ozzie announced to his mother with great importance.

"Really? Are you going to help me clean house?" Mrs. Sims asked with surprise.

"Oh, no. Did you want me to?" asked Ozzie unhappily. That would interrupt his plans dreadfully.

"Not really," said Mrs. Sims. "But what are you planning to clean?"

"Did you know Mrs. Menzer has an old chicken coop in her backyard? I just found out, and she said I could make it into a clubhouse."

"A chicken coop clubhouse?" Ozzie's mother asked in amazement. "Are you sure you won't be bothering Mrs. Menzer?"

"No, no. She said it was okay. You could call her and see for yourself," said Ozzie. He rushed into the kitchen and pulled out the bottle of window cleaner from the cabinet under the sink. He wished his father was home so he could share the news about the chicken coop with him, too.

Loaded down with cleaning apparatus, Ozzie returned to Mrs. Menzer's backyard. He removed the wood from the chicken coop and put the pieces in a corner of his neighbor's garage. Then he dusted every part of the coop. It was so dirty that his eyes began to tear and he sneezed a great deal while he was working. There were lots of spiderwebs. It was a good thing he wasn't afraid of insects, he thought, as a huge spider escaped up the wall Ozzie was cleaning.

When he was sweeping the floor, Ozzie found a penny stuck between two of the floorboards. He picked it up with great delight. It could be something old and rare. The coin was so dark with age that Ozzie couldn't make out the date. He ran to tell Mrs. Menzer about his find and to check if he could keep it. It was only a penny, but he had found it on her property. By rights it belonged to her, and there was always the chance that underneath the grime was something very valuable.

"That coin must have been there for years," said Mrs. Menzer when Ozzie showed it to her.

"I can't read the date," complained Ozzie, squinting at the coin in his hand.

"I know how to fix that," declared Mrs. Menzer.

"I just read about a little trick in one of my magazines." She invited Ozzie into her house. Ozzie watched, puzzled, as she removed a bottle of ketchup from her kitchen cupboard.

"You put a little of this between your thumb and your first finger, with the penny in the middle. Then you rub the ketchup all over the coin with your fingers. It's supposed to clean it perfectly."

This ketchup method seemed strange to Ozzie, but amazingly, within a few seconds the profile of Abraham Lincoln was clearly visible. He ran some cold water on the penny and, sure enough, now he could easily read the year the coin had been minted: 1976.

"That's the year of the bicentennial," said Mrs. Menzer. "My husband was alive then. He must have lost it when he was feeding the chickens."

"I don't need it for my collection," said Ozzie, holding out the penny to his neighbor.

"Keep it anyhow," said Mrs. Menzer. "It was an important year in American history. Maybe it will bring you luck."

"Thanks. And thanks for teaching me your trick," said Ozzie. He was already planning to "ketchupize" all the pennies in his collection at home when he got a chance.

Ozzie returned to the chicken coop and finished sweeping the floor. He looked carefully, but unfortunately he didn't find any more coins. Next he turned his attention to the lone window. He stood on one of the chairs to wash it. He squirted the window cleaner on the pane of glass and then rubbed it very gently so as not to break the already-cracked piece of glass. When he finished inside, he took the chair outdoors and repeated the process from the other side. By the time he had finished all these chores, Ozzie had a lot of dirt on himself. However, there was a big improvement in the cleanliness of the little shed.

Ozzie got up and walked around the inside of the clubhouse. It didn't take long to walk around the four corners. The whole place was no larger than the bathroom at his home. Once the table was here, there would be even less room for walking about. Ozzie looked down at the floor. Even swept clean, the old wooden boards were gray and worn. He remembered that his mother had a piece of old carpeting in the basement. It would look great on the floor, he thought.

By four o'clock, the carpeting was down on the chicken coop's floor and the table was up from Mrs. Menzer's basement. Inside the coop,

Ozzie sat at the table with his library book, a can of fruit juice with a straw, a pad of paper, and a pencil.

It was good that his clubhouse was located so close to his home, because Ozzie counted that he had made more than half a dozen trips back and forth within the last hour. He had gone home for a picture of Babar that hung in his bedroom. He decided that the picture would make the walls look more cheerful. Once he had the picture, he needed to go back for a hammer and a nail. When he stood on the chair to hammer the nail into the wall, he dropped the nail and it fell through a crack in the floor. So then he had to go home for another nail. He returned with three nails, just in case. The next time, however, he was successful. With the nail in place, he was able to hang his picture.

Next Ozzie went home and returned the hammer and lugged back the piece of carpet. Then he decided that he wanted his library book. But when he was in the clubhouse with the library book, he remembered he had wanted to use some of his time writing riddles and jokes. So he went home for a pad of paper and a pencil. From all that running back and forth, he discovered that he was thirsty. So of course he had to go home for something to drink.

So far, Ozzie had only created one new chicken riddle:

What do you do when you see a hundred-pound chicken with horns and sharp teeth?
Run away.

Ozzie wasn't quite satisfied with this riddle. After all, chickens never had horns or teeth. Still, it was the best he could come up with on this hot afternoon.

Ozzie looked down at his notepad. He didn't have any other ideas for new riddles. He sat looking about him. The little clubhouse was almost perfect, but he had a feeling that something was still missing. He felt as if he had forgotten something. But he couldn't figure out what it was.

3
The Missing Ingredient

Mrs. Sims paid Ozzie a visit in the chicken coop in the late afternoon.

"Oh, goody!" exclaimed Ozzie when he saw her. "Did you come to see my clubhouse?"

"Well, that and to give you a message, too," his mother said as she looked around at his new space. "Dad just phoned. We've been invited to join the Rolands and some friends of theirs who have a little boat. We're going to take a short boat ride and then have supper out together."

"Wow! A boat! This is really my lucky day!" said Ozzie, excited at the prospect of the evening ahead of him.

"Well, not exactly," said his mother. "The invitation was for Dad and me, not you."

"Not me?" Ozzie asked incredulously. "Why not? I thought the Rolands liked me."

"Of course they like you," Mrs. Sims assured him. "But sometimes grown-ups want to get together without any children around. I've arranged for Jeff Landers to come and baby-sit this evening. So you'll have to come home and have some supper now."

"Baby-sit!" Ozzie was horrified at the thought. "I never have baby-sitters!" he reminded his mother.

"That's not true. Now that Joan and Steve and Roz live in the other part of our house, there's always someone to keep an eye on you if Dad and I decide to go off somewhere. But before they lived here, you often had baby-sitters."

"I don't like Jeff Landers. He never wants to play any games or anything. All he does is sit and watch our TV," Ozzie protested.

"For one evening you can sit and watch with him," said his mother. "He was the only person I could get. Lizzy Truebell and Amanda Lee are both working out of town as camp counselors."

"I wanted to show Dad my clubhouse." Ozzie pouted. "Can he come and look at it first, before you go out?"

"No," said his mother. "The Rolands are picking me up in their car in an hour, and Dad is going to meet us at the boat marina. Don't worry. This place won't run away. This morning you didn't even know it existed."

"It's not fair," said Ozzie grumpily. He kicked a pebble across Mrs. Menzer's backyard as he reluctantly followed his mother home. All the pleasure of the afternoon was temporarily forgotten because of the disappointment he felt now. It didn't seem fair at all.

The next morning, Ozzie woke in a better mood. He had overslept, so he had missed seeing his father. But now that he was awake, he couldn't wait to return to his clubhouse. Maybe today he could think of even more ways to fix up and improve the chicken coop. And this evening he could show it off to his father. By then it would be better than ever.

True to his word, he walked Samantha for Mrs. Menzer.

He spent part of the morning pushing the table from one corner to another in the clubhouse, trying to decide which was the best arrangement. He read two chapters in his library book and he made up a new riddle:

What did the chicken say when it laid a
square egg?
Ouch.

After he wrote it out, Ozzie wasn't sure if he had
really made that one up. Maybe he had heard it
somewhere before and only thought he had just
made it up.

He tried again:

Do you know the difference between a
chicken and an elephant?
If the answer is no, you'll never get a job at
the zoo.

When his stomach told him it was lunchtime,
Ozzie ran home to get something to eat. "Tomorrow can I take a picnic with me?" he asked.

"Sure," agreed Mrs. Sims. "Are you keeping
busy?"

"Yes," said Ozzie, eating the omelette his
mother had prepared for him. It was true: He had
been so busy ever since he started his chicken coop
club that he hardly remembered to miss Roz.

In the afternoon, however, after he returned
from taking Samantha for her walk, time began to

drag. It was hot in the clubhouse and Ozzie wished he had an electric fan to cool himself off. He began to wish that Roz was sitting across from him on the other chair. He had been so happy setting up the club, but it would be even more fun if Roz was there, too. Maybe he should write her a letter and invite her to be a member right now. In any event, he should share the news about the club with her.

He turned to a clean page in his pad and bit on his pencil as he thought.

"Ozzie?" a voice called him.

He looked up. Mrs. Menzer was standing at the doorway of the chicken coop. "Would you be able to mail a couple of letters for me?" she asked. "I forgot to give them to you when you walked Samantha."

"Sure," said Ozzie. "It's funny that you have letters to mail. I was just going to write a letter, too— to Roz. But I can do it later."

Ozzie was pleased to have an errand to perform for his neighbor. He wanted to do lots of things to help her besides walking Samantha. It was the least he could do in return for the use of the old chicken coop. Besides, he admitted to himself, he was starting to feel restless. He liked having a clubhouse, but he was beginning to realize that just spending time in it wasn't quite enough. After all, he had a bedroom at home that he could have pretended was a clubhouse. As Ozzie walked toward the mailbox, he thought about his chicken coop club. A real club needed something more than just a place to meet.

Ozzie started making a list in his head. A club needed rules. He would have to make some up. What else did a club need? He was still trying to puzzle it out when he reached the mailbox. He dropped the letters in, and as he was about to turn back toward Mrs. Menzer's, Ozzie saw two kids, a boy and a girl, coming in his direction from Kinkade Avenue.

Ozzie knew almost everyone in his neighborhood, by sight, if not by name. But he didn't recognize these two. They were obviously returning from buying ice cream, because they were each busily licking cones. Ozzie looked at them. He wondered who they were and where they lived.

"Hi," the boy said, startling Ozzie. They didn't even know each other and still the boy had greeted him. Ozzie looked at the chocolate ice cream on the boy's chin. It was melting down the sides of his cone and onto his hands, too. He was smaller than

Ozzie, which made Ozzie less shy about responding to him.

"Hi," said Ozzie.

"Want a lick?" the smaller boy offered, holding out his dripping cone toward Ozzie.

"Ryan, you shouldn't do that. You could get germs," scolded the girl who was with him.

"That's okay," said Ozzie. "I have money to get my own ice cream." He felt in his pocket, but the coins that Mrs. Menzer had given him the day before were in the dirty shorts that he had put into the laundry yesterday evening when he got ready for bed.

At a loss for what to say or do next, Ozzie turned to his store of riddles. "Do you know why the farmer put suntan lotion on his chicken?" he asked.

Ryan shook his head. "Nope. I don't believe it. The feathers would get all sticky."

"Because he wanted his meat to be dark but not burned," Ozzie responded.

"How would that turn the meat dark?" asked Ryan.

"It would get a suntan. That would make it dark," Ozzie explained.

"That's dumb," said the girl.

"I don't understand," said Ryan.

"Well, here's another riddle. See if you under-stand this one," said Ozzie. "I saw a chicken egg that was bigger than an elephant. Can you beat that?"

"No, but I saw a duck egg once," said Ryan.

"That's not the answer," said Ozzie. "You're supposed to say, 'Yes, with an eggbeater.'"

"You mean it was a joke?" asked Ryan. "I didn't get it. Do you know any knock-knock jokes? I like that kind."

"Ryan, we're not supposed to talk to strangers," the older girl complained. She had finished her ice cream and was wiping her fingers with a napkin.

"Kids aren't strangers; grown-ups are," Ryan protested.

"My name is Oscar Sims, but everyone calls me Ozzie. I live two blocks from here, on Corn Street," said Ozzie, identifying himself. He suddenly real-ized that he was in the midst of making a friend. For someone as clever and resourceful as he was, he had never been very good at that. It was one of the reasons he clung to his niece, Roz, so much. She was a ready-made friend, whether she liked it or not.

"We live right here," said Ryan, pointing to the

house they were standing in front of. "We just moved here on July first."

"What grade are you in?" Ozzie wanted to know. "I'm going into third grade in September."

"Second," said Ryan. "This is my sister, Ditto. She's going into fifth grade. She's nine and a half."

"I'm nine and a half, but I prefer to be considered ten," Ditto corrected her brother.

"I have a white mouse named Snow White. Do you want to see it?" asked the younger boy.

"Ryan, leave that disgusting thing where it is," said Ditto. "He won it in a raffle at our old school and my mother and I hate it," she told Ozzie.

"What kind of name is Ditto?" Ozzie asked.

"My name is really Elizabeth Louise Richards, just like my mother. Her name is Elizabeth Louise Richards, too. 'Ditto' is my nickname. But it's a very special nickname because it's a Latin word meaning 'the same as before.'"

"My sister knows Latin," said Ozzie. "She'd probably know all about it."

"How old is your sister?" asked Ryan.

"She's twenty-eight," said Ozzie. "Actually, she's only my half sister. We have the same mother but not the same father. And she's married already and has a daughter named Roz who is my best friend and my niece at the same time. Roz is nine and a half, like Ditto."

"Wow," said Ditto. For the first time she was impressed.

"Where is Roz?" asked Ryan. "Maybe we could all play together."

"No, we can't, because Roz is in England. She went away for the whole summer and she won't be back for more than seven weeks." He paused a moment, thinking. "But we could play together—just the three of us in the meantime," he offered. Roz would be proud of him, he thought. She was always urging him to make new friends.

"Okay," said Ryan. "You want to play in our backyard?"

"No," said Ozzie. Suddenly he knew what had been missing at his club. A real club couldn't have just one member and a mascot. A real club needed several people in it. Maybe, if he decided he liked them enough, Ryan and Ditto could become members.

"I have a clubhouse," said Ozzie, feeling very important. "If you want, I'll let you see it."

"A clubhouse. Wow! That's great," said Ryan.

He pulled at his sister. "Let's go," he said.

"Where is it?" asked Ditto suspiciously. "Is it up a tree, like a tree house?"

"No. It's on the ground," said Ozzie, guessing that Ditto didn't like heights. "Actually, it used to be a chicken coop, so I call my club the Chicken Coop Club."

"I never belonged to a club," said Ryan.

"Me neither," said Ozzie. "That's why I started this one."

"We'll have to ask our mother," said Ditto. She went into the house and came out a minute later with a grown-up version of herself.

"Where do you live, Ozzie?" Mrs. Richards asked.

Ozzie explained where he lived and that the clubhouse was just a couple of houses away from his home.

"It sounds like fun," said Ditto.

Ryan's mother smiled at Ozzie. "All right, kids. You can go. But be sure and be home by five."

Ditto looked at her wristwatch. "That means we'll have an hour and a half," she told her brother. She looked at Ozzie. "Could I bring Candy to the clubhouse?" she asked.

"Sure," said Ozzie. What a great thing—in just

a couple of minutes he'd mailed Mrs. Menzer's letters, found two possible new members for his club, and been offered candy besides. He wondered what kind of candy Ditto was going to get.

Ditto ran to the house next door to hers. A minute later she came back with another girl. Ozzie had seen the girl around before. She didn't go to his school. She went to St. Agnes, a parochial school, where she wore a special uniform.

"Hi," said the new girl shyly. "My name's Candy, Candy Henderson."

Ozzie looked at her and thought about what he had done. He had gotten himself three visitors to his club. But two of them were girls older than he was. They'd probably want to boss him around the way Roz liked to do. And there wasn't any candy at all.

4
The First Meeting of the Chicken Coop Club

The first thing that Ozzie realized as he walked inside his clubhouse followed by Ryan, Ditto, and Candy was how small the place was. It had been small before, but the presence of three more people made it seem to shrink still smaller.

Ditto seemed to agree. "This is very little for a club," she said as she pushed past Ozzie to look around.

"If it's too small for you, you can go home," said Ozzie. He was hurt by her criticism, even if what she had to say was the very thing he had been thinking.

"I didn't say it was *too* small," Ditto responded quickly.

"It's cozy," said Candy.

"It has a funny smell," Ditto noted next.

"You can go home if you don't like the smell," said Ozzie. He had noticed the unusual odor inside the coop when he had first entered it. But by now he had grown accustomed to it and it didn't bother him.

"I didn't say it was a *bad* smell," Ditto protested. "It's just different."

"My mom has an air spray that she uses to make our house smell good," Candy said. "I could bring it and make this whole clubhouse smell like a flower garden."

"Those sprays are bad for the environment," said Ozzie. "I saw a program about that on TV."

"Well, my mom doesn't use it very much," said Candy.

"There are other ways to make this place smell better," Ditto offered. "I could bring a bunch of flowers and put them in a vase on the table. How about that?" she asked Ozzie.

"Can you open the window?" asked Ryan.

Ozzie hadn't tried to do that. Now he climbed up on one of the chairs and gave a push. The window opened a little, but when he removed his hand, it slid shut again.

"Here," said Ryan. He handed up the library

book that Ozzie had left on the table. *Remember the Alamo* was the title.

"You can't take a book to prop open a window," said Ozzie, amazed that Ryan would think of using a book that way. "I'll look around later for a block of wood or something like that."

The window remained closed as he climbed off the chair and offered it to Candy. "Ryan and I can sit on the floor," Ozzie said.

"Can we be members of your club?" asked Ditto when they were all seated. "I'd like to be in a club."

"Me too," said Ryan. "Can I join?"

"I've always wanted to be in a club," said Candy. "Does your club have a name?"

"I call this the Chicken Coop Club," Ozzie told her.

"Then you have to let me join, because of my name."

"Candy?" Ozzie was puzzled.

"Henderson!" said Candy, smiling at him. "I'm Candy Henderson. I've got a chicken in my name."

Ozzie grinned with delight. He had a feeling that Candy would be a good club member and a good friend. *Hen*derson. He liked that.

"What about us?" asked Ryan. "We can't help it if our name is Richards. We like chicken. In fact,

my dad barbecued some on our grill last night for supper."

"And we had leftover chicken for lunch," added Ditto.

"Do you like chicken jokes?" asked Ozzie.

"I don't know any," said Ditto.

"But if we did, we'd like them," said Ryan.

"It will be more fun if there are four of us," Candy pointed out. "There are more games that we can play and more things that we can do."

"You can be president," said Ditto.

Ozzie hadn't thought about that. But of course he would be president of a club that he had started and organized. And if he was president, no one could boss him around. In fact, so far neither of the girls had even tried, he realized happily.

"All right," Ozzie agreed. "You can all be members of my club. And when Roz comes back home, she'll be in the club, too." He tried to think of what other pronouncements he should make at this moment when his club was being officially established.

"This chicken coop belongs to Mrs. Menzer. And she has a dog named Samantha. Samantha is the club mascot."

"What about Snow White?" asked Ryan. "Can't she be our mascot, too?"

"Yuck," said Ditto. "One mascot is enough. We don't need that mouse for a mascot, too."

"Let's vote," said Candy. "All in favor of having two mascots, raise your hand."

Ryan's hand shot up. Ozzie thought it would be neat to have a mouse mascot as well as Samantha. His hand went up, too. Candy raised her hand as well. "She's not so bad," she said to Ditto. "I don't know why you don't like her."

"I hate mice," said Ditto, shuddering. But she had been outvoted. Snow White had just been elected co-mascot of the Chicken Coop Club.

By the time Ditto noticed on her watch that she and Ryan had to go home for supper, they had settled several other issues as well. They had devised a club handshake and discussed a secret password. Ozzie suggested *Cock-a-doodle-doo*.

Ditto protested that only roosters made that sound. "Female chickens go *cluck, cluck, cluck*," she said.

"All right," Ozzie agreed. "The girls will say one thing and the boys the other. We'll meet back here at nine o'clock tomorrow morning."

"I'll ask my mother if we can bring a picnic," offered Ditto.

As they left the clubhouse, Candy suddenly shouted out. "Stop. I just remembered. I know a chicken joke."

"What is it?" asked Ozzie eagerly.

"Why did the chicken say *bowwow, meow, oink-oink,* and *moooo?*"

"Why?" asked Ryan.

"She was studying foreign languages at school," said Candy. "Get it?"

"No," said Ryan.

"That's okay. I do," said Ozzie. He realized that Ryan was only just out of first grade, so you couldn't expect him to understand everything. He was still a nice kid.

"Cock-a-doodle-doo. See you tomorrow," he called as his three club mates started off toward their homes.

"Cluck, cluck," called Candy Henderson.

"Cluck, cluck," called Ditto.

"Cluck, cluck." Ryan echoed the girls. But Ditto gave her brother a poke and whispered in his ear.

"Cock-a-doodle-doo," Ryan corrected himself.

Ozzie went around to the front of the house

to offer to walk Samantha one more time. He thought he ought to explain to Mrs. Menzer about the other members of his club. She was a nice lady, so he didn't think she would object. Maybe he ought to make her an honorary member as well. After all, the chicken coop was located in her yard. He wondered if she would be willing to call out "Cluck, cluck" whenever she saw him. No. He didn't think he would ask her to do that.

5
Mr. Sims Is Tired

The afternoon had been filled with so many un-expected events that Ozzie was more excited than ever. He could hardly wait till his father came home from work so he could share it all with him. He was due home any minute.

"So now there are four members in the Chicken Coop Club," Ozzie reported to his mother. He was helping her by trimming the ends off some string beans as he spoke. "We made up a secret handshake and a secret password. You can't get into the clubhouse unless you say the right thing."

"What about Mrs. Menzer?" asked his mother.

"She doesn't know them," said Ozzie. He

thought for a moment. "Do you think I should teach them to her?"

"No. What does she think of having so many kids in and out of her yard?"

"She said it was nice to hear us laughing," said Ozzie. He remembered how the four club members had sat around inside the coop. He remembered the riddle that Candy had asked.

"Why did the chicken say *moo, oink, meow,* and *bowwow?*" he asked his mother now.

"He was confused?" asked Mrs. Sims, taking the string beans from Ozzie and putting them into a pot. "I have no idea. Maybe your father will know."

Ozzie heard his father's car in the driveway and ran to the door.

"Dad? Why did the chicken say *moo, oink, meow,* and *bowwow?*" he called, running outside to greet him as he got out of his car.

"Beats me," answered his father, rubbing his hand on Ozzie's head by way of saying hello.

"Make a guess," Ozzie urged.

"I can't. I'm too tired for riddles just now. Maybe a little later."

"Oh," said Ozzie, disappointed. His father always gave him good answers, even if they were the wrong ones. Then Ozzie remembered all his news. "Dad, I have a club and a clubhouse and three new members and even two club mascots."

"That's great," said his father, going in the door. He removed his necktie and sat down.

"Are you all right?" asked Ozzie's mother, looking at her husband.

"Why do you ask?" said Mr. Sims.

"You look exhausted," she said, bending to kiss him. "It must be this hot weather."

"Dad, come and see the clubhouse," said Ozzie, grabbing his father by the arm.

"Not now," said his father. "I guess it *is* the heat. I'm really feeling too tired to go anywhere."

"But it isn't far. It's just in Mrs. Menzer's backyard," Ozzie said, still holding on to his father's arm. "We could be there in a minute."

"Ozzie, leave your father be. I'm getting you a cold drink," Ozzie's mother said to her husband. "Maybe the sugar in some fruit juice will help revive you."

"But Dad," Ozzie protested. "Supper's still cooking. We could go to the clubhouse and be back home in about two minutes." It was hard for him to understand his father's reluctance.

Even with his son's urging, Mr. Sims made no effort to get up.

"I've been waiting for you all day," nagged Ozzie. "You weren't here to see it yesterday. The least you could do would be to come with me now."

"Ozzie," Mrs. Sims scolded. "Calm down. That old chicken coop has been in Mrs. Menzer's yard for years and years. If your father doesn't see it tonight, he can see it tomorrow."

"He doesn't even care about my clubhouse," said Ozzie, feeling sorry for himself. "He probably won't want to come tomorrow, either."

"We'll go after supper," said Ozzie's father in a weary voice.

Somehow supper was not the cheerful meal it usually was. Ozzie didn't know if it was because his mother was serving flounder, which was one of his least-favorite dishes. The white fish looked so boring on his plate. And it tasted boring in his mouth, too. Maybe he was more aware of the food than usual because his parents weren't talking very much. Most evenings they joked and laughed a lot while they ate. There was cantaloupe for dessert tonight. That was pretty boring, too. "Don't you have any cookies or ice cream?" Ozzie complained to his mother.

"It's too hot for baking cookies," she answered. "Besides, it's healthier to eat a piece of fruit for dessert."

Ozzie frowned. He wished his mother wasn't a nurse. He bet other mothers didn't worry so much about what was healthy and what wasn't.

After supper, Mr. Sims sprawled out on the living room sofa and watched the news. Ozzie thought they'd go over to the clubhouse as soon as the news was over. But the sky, which had been somewhat overcast in the late afternoon, became suddenly much darker. Ozzie could hear the sound of thunder in the distance. Then he heard and smelled the rain.

Mrs. Sims went around checking the open windows to see that rain wasn't coming into the house. "You can show Dad your clubhouse tomorrow," she told Ozzie, "when he's feeling better."

Ozzie felt overwhelmed with disappointment. If his mother had urged him, his father would have gone to the clubhouse before supper. Now the sky was so dark that it would be hard to see very much inside the chicken coop. He felt like kicking something. This made two evenings in a row that he hadn't been able to show off his clubhouse. It wasn't at all like his father to lie around on the sofa and not pay attention to Ozzie.

"Why don't you write a letter to Roz," suggested his mother. "You can tell her about all the things that have been happening."

Ozzie wasn't really in the mood now for writing a letter. But on the other hand, even if his father didn't care about his clubhouse, he was sure that Roz would be interested. So he got a sheet of paper and started writing.

By bedtime, Ozzie had written a two-page letter. It was the longest one yet. His last letter had been really just a couple of chicken riddles. There hadn't been any news to report. This time, Ozzie had so much to share with Roz that he didn't even bother to write any riddles at all. Mrs. Sims had stocked up on airmail stamps when her daughter and family went off to England. So the letter to Roz was in its envelope with the stamp on it, all ready for mailing.

Ozzie's father was still sprawled on the sofa. Now he was watching some sort of documentary. "Good night, Dad," Ozzie called as he started up to bed.

"Night, Ozzie," Mr. Sims responded. "I'm sorry

I didn't get to see your clubhouse. I'll see it tomorrow."

"Promise?" asked Ozzie.

"It's a promise," his father said. "Cross my heart and hope to die."

It was not a promise Mr. Sims could keep. In the middle of the night, Ozzie woke, aware that he heard unusual sounds coming from outside. Though the shade was pulled down on his window, he could see a flashing light from the street. Groggily he got out of bed and pulled up the shade. In front of his house, he saw an ambulance, its motor running. He rubbed his eyes and wondered if he was having a dream. Has there been an accident? Or is somebody sick? he asked himself. Then he saw his mother, in her bathrobe, standing near the back of the ambulance. She was talking with an attendant. Ozzie couldn't hear what she was saying, so he decided to go and see what had happened.

There were lights on all over the house. He squinted as his eyes adjusted to the brightness. When he glanced at the clock in the living room, he saw that it was 3:20 in the morning. It was the first time in his life he had been awake at this hour, he thought to himself. The front door of the house was open. And even though he was barefoot and in pajamas, Ozzie walked outside. Just as he put his foot down on the damp brick walk, the ambulance door was slammed shut and the driver began to pull away from the curb.

Mrs. Sims turned to the house and saw her son. "Ozzie," she said, putting her arms around him and hugging him tightly. "I hoped we wouldn't wake you."

"What's going on?" Ozzie asked, puzzled.

"The emergency medical people are taking Dad to the hospital. He has some bad pains."

"Couldn't you take care of him?" asked Ozzie. His father always said that he had been so smart to marry a nurse.

"It may be nothing. I hope it's nothing," said Mrs. Sims in a strained voice. "But just in case, it's better to be in the hospital, where they have all the best equipment." She looked down at Ozzie's bare feet.

"Come on inside," she said. "I don't want you getting sick, too."

Mrs. Sims walked upstairs with Ozzie, turning off the lights as they went.

"What do you think's the matter with Dad?"

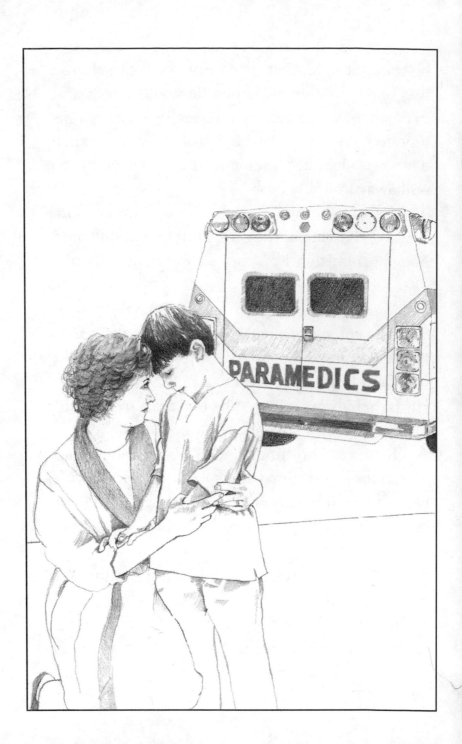

Ozzie asked her anxiously. He remembered how tired his father had been in the evening.

"Hopefully nothing," said Mrs. Sims. "But sometimes what seems like simple indigestion is really something else. Try to go back to sleep. Most likely, in the morning we'll be laughing about all this drama in the middle of the night."

Ozzie lay down on his bed and tried to figure out what could be wrong with his father. What was the something else that only seemed like indigestion?

The next thing he knew, bright light was coming into his window. He turned his pillow over and pulled the sheet over himself. Why was his shade up? he wondered. Vaguely he recalled that during the night he had been out of bed and pulled it up. Why had he done that?

All at once he remembered. "Mom?" he shouted, running from the bedroom. It wasn't a dream. During the night his father had been taken to the hospital.

Ozzie found his mother in the kitchen, talking on the phone. She was wearing jeans and a shirt, but her hair hadn't been combed yet and there were dark rings under her eyes. She looked old and tired.

"All right. Yes. Of course, I understand," she said. "Thanks very much. I'll see you in a little while." She hung up the phone and noticed Ozzie.

"How's Dad?" asked Ozzie.

Mrs. Sims put her arms around Ozzie and hugged him tightly. "It's good he got to the hospital last night," she said. "He had a heart attack."

Ozzie didn't know much about medicine, but he had heard about heart attacks. They were very bad.

"Will he be okay?" he asked.

"I think so," said his mother. "That was Connie Hearne. I've worked with her at the hospital. She said the doctor was examining him now. They have all sorts of wonderful tests these days. They'll be able to assess just how much damage was done to the heart muscle and how best to treat it."

Mrs. Sims got up from the chair where she had been sitting and opened the refrigerator. She poured a glass of orange juice for herself and one for Ozzie. "I'm going to go over to the hospital. I spoke with Mrs. Menzer. She's going to keep an eye on you this morning while I'm away. Don't give her any trouble or get into mischief," she instructed Ozzie.

"When can Dad come home?" Ozzie wanted to know.

"It will depend on how severe his attack was. There's always the possibility that they will want to operate on him."

"Operate?" asked Ozzie. Operations were serious things.

"Maybe not," said Mrs. Sims. "Probably not. They can do a lot with diet and exercise, too. Don't worry."

Ozzie reached for his glass of juice and took a sip. Suddenly the words his father had said to him before he went to sleep last night came back to him: *Cross my heart and hope to die.* Ozzie put down his glass. The orange juice didn't taste the way it usually did. It seemed bitter. The fact was, he wasn't thirsty and he wasn't hungry this morning. How could he just eat his breakfast and go out to play while his father was in the hospital? It was all right for his mother to tell him to keep out of mischief, but when she said, "Don't worry," he didn't think he could obey that instruction. He knew he was going to be worrying every minute of the day. Tears filled his eyes as he thought about his father.

The letter he had written the night before to Roz was lying on the counter. Ozzie picked it up and looked at it through his tears. "I'd better write another letter and tell Roz. She'll want to know about Dad," he said.

"Oh no. Don't do that," said Mrs. Sims. "There's absolutely no point in worrying Roz and Joan and Steve. There's nothing they can do and the news will just upset them. By the time they come home at the end of the summer, everything will be just fine," said Ozzie's mother.

"You mean we're just going to pretend that everything's okay?" asked Ozzie. He was shocked at his mother's plan.

"Yes," said Mrs. Sims. "Promise me that when you write your next letter, you won't say anything about your father. Just write about yourself. Write about your new club."

Ozzie realized that he had forgotten all about his club. Yesterday it had been the most exciting and the most important thing in his life. And now, with his father in the hospital, he didn't care about it at all. Furthermore, he was sure that his mother's decision about not informing Roz and her parents was the wrong way to react at a time like this.

Mr. Sims's words of the night before kept echoing in Ozzie's head.

Cross my heart and hope to die.

6
Ozzie Gets a Present

Yesterday when he had gone home, Ozzie had never guessed that he would have news to report at the next meeting of the Chicken Coop Club. But even before he could announce that his father was in the hospital, everyone knew.

Mrs. Menzer stood waiting for Ozzie outside the little shed. When he arrived, she threw her arms around him and kissed the top of his head. Then in a teary voice, she said, "Don't worry, Ozzie. I'm sure your father will be fine."

If Ozzie hadn't already been worried, Mrs. Menzer's unexpected show of affection would have reinforced his feeling that his father's illness was serious. Mrs. Menzer had never kissed him before.

"My husband died of a heart attack," Mrs. Menzer said sadly. "But nowadays the doctors can do so much more than they could in the past."

Ozzie felt his stomach lurch at the information about Mr. Menzer. He had never known the man, but now that he was using his chicken coop, he felt a bond to him. As he took Samantha for her morning walk, Ozzie discovered that his thoughts were full of Mr. Menzer. Had he gotten sick in the middle of the night the way his father had? Did he go off in an ambulance? Did he die in the hospital? By the time he got back to the clubhouse, he was very close to tears.

A minute later, when Ditto, Ryan, and Candy arrived together, laughing and laden down with supplies for the clubhouse, Mrs. Menzer stopped them to announce the news about Ozzie's father.

Mrs. Menzer's presence and her news distracted the members from the rules they had set up the day before. By rights, Ozzie, who had arrived first, should have demanded the secret password from each of the others before letting them come in.

"Is he very sick?" asked Ditto when the four kids were inside the clubhouse. A calendar she had brought for the wall and a cooler and a shopping bag filled with other items for the club were on the table. But this was not the moment for housekeeping.

The news of Ozzie's father was such a distraction that they hardly noticed the damp patch on the rug where the roof had leaked during the rainstorm yesterday evening.

"I don't know," said Ozzie. He found a dry place and sat down on the floor. "Everyone says not to worry. But I can't help worrying. My mother said she'd know more to tell me when she gets home from the hospital today." He paused and then decided that it was all right to admit how he felt to the club members. After all, what was the point of secret passwords and secret handshakes if you couldn't confide your secret feelings to one another?

"I'm scared," said Ozzie, half-whispering his fears. "I'm scared he's going to die."

"My mom said that I shouldn't worry about her dying," said Candy, trying to reassure Ozzie. "She said parents hardly ever die until they're very, very, very old. And by then I'll be all grown-up. She said that most likely I'd be married and have children of my own by then." Candy giggled. "So you don't have to worry. I bet your dad will be okay."

"Yeah," said Ozzie, trying to convince himself that this was so. "Do you know how old your father is?"

"Thirty-four," said Candy. "And my mother is thirty-two."

"Our parents are older than that," said Ditto. "Our mother is thirty-five and our father is thirty-nine."

"Wow," said Candy, sounding impressed. "Thirty-nine is almost forty. That's pretty old."

"Our grandmother is going to be eighty," announced Ryan. "That's *very* old."

"Will you go to the hospital to see your dad?" asked Ditto. "Ryan and I went to the hospital and visited our dad when he was in a car accident last year. He was a mess. He had bandages all over and two black eyes, like he'd been in a fight. He said he was lucky that it wasn't worse. But he sure looked pretty bad to me."

"He meant that he could have been killed," said Ryan.

Ozzie blinked away the tears that were forming in his eyes. He knew his friends were trying hard to say things to cheer him up. But everything they said just made him feel worse. In the first place, it had never bothered him before that his parents were older than the parents of his classmates at school. He'd never even thought about the chance of them dying just because they were old. Ozzie knew that his father was fifty-six years old. That was seventeen years older than Ryan and Ditto's father. And his mother was old, too. She was fifty-one. The thought that they were really ancient and close to death came as a shock to him.

Furthermore, Ozzie had something else to worry about. Hearing about Ryan and Ditto's father's accident made him think about his mother. Every time she got into the car and drove to the hospital, there was the possibility that she could be killed. He'd read stories and seen movies about kids who were orphans, but it had never occurred to Ozzie that he could suddenly become one, too. It would be terrible to lose his parents and to be on his own in the world. Ozzie's eyes burned with tears.

Ditto noticed and changed the subject. "My mom packed a picnic for Ryan and me, but there's enough for all four of us. So when it's lunchtime, we can eat right here. We won't have to go home."

"Could I have something to eat now?" asked

Ryan. He pushed the catch to open the cooler.

"You just had breakfast," complained Ditto. But she pulled out a package wrapped in aluminum foil and passed around some brownies that her mother had meant for dessert.

Ozzie automatically took one. Even though he hadn't eaten any breakfast, he wasn't really hungry. He nibbled on the brownie to be polite. He knew his mother would not be pleased to see him eating sweets at this hour. Besides, how could he eat while his father was in the hospital?

"Why did the chicken eat brownies for breakfast?" he asked.

"He was hungry?" said Ryan, his own mouth full of brownie.

Ozzie shook his head. "Because he couldn't wait until lunchtime."

Ryan started laughing. "That's just like us," he said with delight.

It was nice to have someone appreciate the riddle he'd just made up. Roz usually groaned and complained about them. And though his parents always laughed, Ozzie sometimes wondered if they really thought his jokes were good ones. Maybe they just thought it was one of their parental duties to laugh at their son's chicken riddles and jokes.

"I just remembered something," said Ryan, and he jumped up from the floor.

"Where are you going?" asked Ditto as Ryan ran out the door.

"I'll be right back," said Ryan.

Ditto shrugged her shoulders. "Maybe he had to go to the bathroom," she explained in apology for her brother's unexpected behavior.

"Look what I brought for the clubhouse," said Candy. She pulled a plastic wastebasket out of the shopping bag. "We have an old folding chair at home that I'll bring this afternoon," she offered.

Ditto crumpled up the aluminum foil that had been around the brownies and put it into the wastebasket. "You brought it just in time," she complimented Candy.

Then she turned to Ozzie. "I think this calendar should be hung over here." Any other day, Ozzie would have objected to Ditto's bossy behavior. It was his clubhouse. He should be the one to decide where things were hung on the wall. But today he could hardly keep his mind on the doings in the clubhouse. He wished Roz and her parents were around. He wanted to talk to them about his father.

"Here I am," shouted Ryan, coming back into the clubhouse. His face was all red and sweaty from running and he was out of breath. In his hands he carried a cardboard shoe box. There were holes punched in the top.

"Why did you bring that disgusting thing here?" asked his sister.

"I'm going to give it to Ozzie as a present." Ryan handed the box to Ozzie.

"My mother gave him a week to get rid of it," Ditto informed the other club members. "But I didn't know you were going to give it to Ozzie," she said, looking at her brother.

"I didn't know, either," said Ryan. "I didn't even know Ozzie until yesterday. But I think it's a good present and maybe it will make him feel better while his father is in the hospital."

"It wouldn't make *me* feel better to get a mouse," said Ditto. "It would make me feel worse."

"I don't feel worse," said Ozzie, taking the shoe box from Ryan. "Thanks a whole lot," he added.

"I bet my mom is saying, 'Thanks for finally getting rid of that mouse,'" Ditto whispered to Candy.

"Be careful when you open the box," Ryan

warned Ozzie. "Snow White might jump out."

"Let me see," said Candy. She and Ryan hung over Ozzie's shoulders. He put the box on the table and then carefully removed the lid. In a corner of the box hovered a small white mouse. It looked up at Ozzie with its tiny eyes. It sniffed for a moment and then began to run around inside the box.

"Gee," said Ozzie. "This is a neat present. Thanks," he said again.

"Will you let me visit her?" asked Ryan.

"Sure," said Ozzie. "How do you know she's a girl mouse?"

"Well, I don't really," admitted Ryan. "But the kids in my class named her Snow White. And that's a girl's name. We had a mother mouse named Snowball and this was one of her babies. There were also Snowflake, Snowman, and Snowstorm. We didn't know which were boys and which were girls. On the last day of school we had a raffle to see who would keep each of the mice and I won Snow White."

"Thank goodness we didn't get seven dwarf mice as well," said Ditto, laughing at her own joke.

"I'll take good care of her," Ozzie told Ryan. "And you can visit her whenever you want." He removed the little mouse from the shoe box and petted her gently.

He wasn't sure how his mother felt about pet mice. But at least he didn't have to contend with a sister making nasty remarks about his new pet the way Ryan had.

A pet white mouse might be useful for cheering up his father when he came home from the hospital, Ozzie thought. In fact, it occurred to him, if he was allowed to visit at the hospital, maybe he'd take Snow White with him.

7
Snow White
Takes a Trip

In the middle of the afternoon, Mrs. Menzer came calling at the entrance to the chicken coop. The four club members were sitting on the floor, laughing and playing a card game that Candy had taught them. Even Ozzie was distracted enough by the game to stop worrying about his father temporarily.

"Ozzie," Mrs. Menzer called. "Your mother phoned. She just came back from the hospital. She said you should go home."

Ozzie froze. The card in his hand was halted on its way to the pile on the floor.

"Did she say anything else?" Ozzie asked. His voice came out scratchy with emotion as all his fears returned to him.

"Your father is still in intensive care. I guess the next twenty-four hours are very crucial."

Ozzie let out a sigh of relief. His father was still alive! He put the card down and stood up.

"Don't forget Snow White," Ryan reminded Ozzie. The mouse had had a busy day being petted and fed by three out of the four members.

Ozzie picked up the shoe box and hurried home.

Mrs. Sims was waiting at the door. She gave Ozzie a big hug. "So far, so good," she said when Ozzie asked about his father. "They've given him medicines to thin his blood and to break up any clots. Now we just have to wait and hope that everything is working as it should." She sounded much more cheerful than she had in the morning, and Ozzie felt relieved.

"Can I see him?" asked Ozzie.

"He's sleeping now," his mother reported. "But I'm going back to the hospital in a little while and you can come with me. If he's awake, I think they'll let you in the room for a couple of minutes. You'll be good medicine for him, too."

Ozzie nodded.

"I spent half the morning on the telephone," said Mrs. Sims. "I called every sleep-away camp I ever heard of and a good many that I'd never heard of, too. I thought it would be a good idea for you to have a place to spend the next few weeks. I'm going to be running back and forth to the hospital; I may well be there more hours than when I'm actually working. And even when your father comes home, we won't be able to take any small trips with you the way we had planned."

"No," said Ozzie sharply. "I don't want to go away. I want to be here with you, and with Dad when he comes home."

He remembered how his mother had forbidden him to write anything about his father to Roz because it would upset her and her parents. If he went off to camp, his mother wouldn't write and tell him anything, either. Besides, he couldn't just abandon his father.

"Don't worry," said his mother. "None of the places I called had any openings in the middle of the session. Two camps put your name on a waiting list for August. But who knows what the situation will be then. I wanted a place for you to go right now."

"Right now I'm going with you to the hospital," Ozzie reminded his mother.

"Well, in that case, go upstairs and take a

shower first and change your clothes. I don't know what you do over at that chicken coop, but you certainly come home very dirty. I can hardly find your freckles. They're hidden underneath all the grime."

"Look what I have," said Ozzie. He opened a corner of the shoe box to display his new possession.

"Where did you find that?" asked Mrs. Sims, surprised by the unexpected sight of the mouse.

"Ryan gave her to me. Her name's Snow White." He didn't mention that Ryan's mother would not let her son keep the mouse. And luckily for Ozzie, his mother didn't say anything to that effect.

Ozzie put the shoe box in his bedroom and went to get washed. Then he put on a pair of clean slacks and a clean shirt. He heard Snow White scratching about inside her box and remembered that he wanted to show off the mouse to his father. Rather than carry the shoe box with him, he took the mouse out of her home. Carefully and gently, he placed her inside his pocket. He suspected that his mother would object if she saw the box. But if she didn't see it, she wouldn't say anything. And if she didn't forbid it, then it would be all right to take Snow White to the hospital. Luckily his slacks had big baggy pockets.

Ozzie just knew his father would love seeing the white mouse.

Snow White wriggled around a bit in Ozzie's pocket as they drove to the hospital. Ozzie kept his hand in the pocket and could feel the mouse's movements.

"You'll have to stay in the waiting area," Mrs. Sims explained to Ozzie. "I'll check on how Dad is doing. They don't generally permit children to visit, but since I'm on the staff, I'm pretty certain I can arrange for them to make an exception for you."

"I'm not a child," Ozzie protested.

"Anyone under twelve is not allowed to see patients, according to the hospital's regulations," his mother explained.

It was a small satisfaction to Ozzie that if Roz had been in town, she would also be considered too young.

Mrs. Sims parked the car and left Ozzie sitting in the waiting room. "I should have thought to tell you to bring your library book," she said.

"That's okay," said Ozzie.

"I may be gone for quite a while. Don't leave this room."

"Okay," said Ozzie. He looked around. There were two women sitting together in a corner, speaking softly. The other chairs and sofas were empty.

"You could look at the magazines," Ozzie's mother suggested, pointing to a stack on a nearby table.

"Okay," said Ozzie. He was eager for his mother to leave him alone so he could take poor Snow White out of his pocket. The little mouse had probably exhausted all the air that was in there.

"I'll be back as soon as I can," Mrs. Sims said.

Ozzie nodded. He took a seat as far away as possible from the two women in the room. As his mother walked off, he pulled his new pet from his pocket. The mouse stood on Ozzie's lap, twitching her nose and looking about. The hospital looked and smelled very different from both the shoe box and the chicken coop clubhouse. Snow White was probably very confused.

"This is a hospital," Ozzie said softly to the mouse. "My father is in one of the rooms down the hall because he had a heart attack."

"Did you say something?" one of the women across the room called to Ozzie.

"He said his father had a heart attack," said the second woman. She must have very good ears, Ozzie thought. He had whispered the information to Snow White and hadn't expected anyone to be able to hear him.

"Oh, you poor boy," said the first woman. "Is it very serious?"

"A heart attack is always serious," the second woman said to the first.

"Was this his first attack?" asked the first woman.

Ozzie nodded his head.

"My husband had bypass surgery two years ago and the doctor said he's better than new," said the first woman. She had blond hair that was so light, it was almost white.

"It would have been better if he hadn't needed the surgery in the first place," the second woman pointed out. She was wearing sunglasses even though they were inside and there was no sun.

"Well of course it would have been better not to need surgery. But since he had it, it's good that it was so successful. Will your father be operated on?"

"I don't know," said Ozzie. All the time that the

women were talking to him, he was quietly stroking Snow White.

"The operations are serious, but they are becoming so common these days that I don't think you need to worry," said the woman with the blond hair.

"If your husband is okay, how come you're here?" Ozzie asked out of curiosity.

"It's my daughter. She just got a new nose," said the blond woman.

Ozzie let go of Snow White and ran his fingers over his nose. "What happened to her old one?" he asked. He had never known that noses could fall off or wear out.

"She didn't like the way she looked. She wants to be a model and she said that with the nose she was born with, all she could model was shoes."

"What's that?" asked the woman with the sunglasses in an anxious voice.

"What's what?" asked her blond friend.

"Just as you were talking about noses, I thought I saw a nose roll across the floor. I guess it was my imagination."

Ozzie looked down at his lap. Snow White had disappeared. He got down on the floor and started looking under his chair.

"Don't be ridiculous," said the blond woman. "If you insist on wearing your sunglasses indoors, of course you can't see properly."

"Well, I know it can't have been a nose," said the woman with the sunglasses. "But I did see something roll across the floor. Do you see anything?" she asked Ozzie.

Ozzie did not see anything. He wondered where Snow White could have gotten to in such a hurry. He crawled along the floor and looked under each of the chairs. He looked toward the door, but there was no sign of the mouse there, either. He jumped up and closed the door. It wouldn't do for Snow White to go exploring outside this room. The hospital was a huge place and it might take hours for him to locate her if she ran down the hallway.

"You better get off the floor," the blond woman told Ozzie. "Even though this is a hospital, floors are never that clean. You'll probably get filthy, and your mother has enough to worry about with your father. She won't want you getting dirty as well."

"What's a little dirt," said the woman with sunglasses. "He can always take a bath."

"You can talk. You wouldn't even notice if he

was dirty, since you are wearing those dark glasses. But his mother won't be pleased," said the blond woman.

"What do you have against my dark glasses?" her friend asked.

The two women began a discussion about whether or not it was good for your eyes to wear sunglasses indoors. Ozzie kept searching for Snow White. He had to find her before his mother came back.

Just then the door to the waiting area opened. "Why is this door shut?" a voice asked.

Ozzie looked up. He saw a large woman in a nurse's white uniform. It was just like the one his mother wore on the days that she worked at the hospital.

"Are you Oscar Sims?" the nurse asked him.

"Yes," said Ozzie.

"Your mother told me you were here. I'm Edith Millsap. Your mother will be back for you in a little while."

"Thanks," said Ozzie, wishing Nurse Millsap would hurry back to her hospital work.

"I'm leaving this door open," said the nurse. "It shouldn't be closed." She turned to walk away.

"What's that?" she said, pointing to the floor. "I just saw something roll across the floor. It was white."

"See," said the woman with dark glasses to her friend. "I didn't imagine it." She turned to the nurse. "We were talking about Claire's daughter getting a nose job and I thought I saw a nose. I know my eyes were playing tricks on me, but for a fraction of a second, that's what it looked like to me."

"Oscar, do you see anything?" asked Nurse Millsap. Ozzie didn't respond. But in fact, he had seen the same flash of white as Nurse Millsap. Unlike the older women, he had known immediately what it was. What he didn't know was how the nurse and the other two women would react when they realized they had seen a mouse.

Snow White had just run under the leather sofa in the center of the waiting area. He had to catch the mouse before she left to explore underneath yet another piece of furniture. His hand shot out and he moved it all around. Suddenly he felt one of Snow White's tiny little legs. He pulled gently and extracted the leg with the rest of the mouse attached to it.

"Ozzie, what are you doing down there?" a

voice called out. Startled by the unexpected voice of his mother in the doorway, Ozzie let go of Snow White. The mouse took advantage of her returned freedom and instantly sped across the waiting room and out through the open door. Ozzie jumped up from the floor. He pushed past his mother and Nurse Millsap and charged down the hospital hallway after his new pet.

"What's that?" shrieked the blond woman. Her high-pitched voice carried well and Ozzie could hear her even though he was some distance away.

"Ozzie!" Mrs. Sims called, running after her son.

"Ozzie!" called Nurse Millsap, running after Mrs. Sims, who was running after Ozzie.

Snow White paused for a moment. She was probably trying to decide which way to turn. The corridor split off in two directions. Ozzie grabbed the mouse during her moment of indecision and held her tightly. He was not going to let her get loose a second time.

"This is Snow White," he said, holding up the little white mouse and showing her to everyone. Behind his mother and Nurse Millsap, the two women from the waiting room and several other members of the hospital staff had gathered as well.

"You brought a mouse to the hospital?" Nurse Millsap's voice was incredulous. "Do you realize that mice are vermin? They carry germs! And furthermore, if a patient was startled by a mouse running across the floor, he might have a heart attack."

Ozzie looked down at his mouse. She looked so tiny and white and clean, it was hard for him to believe that she was dangerous. A couple of the nurses shook their heads as they turned back to their duties.

"Maybe that mouse will turn into a princess at midnight," said the woman with dark glasses, who had come from the waiting room. She started laughing.

"That's Cinderella, not Snow White," said the blond woman, correcting her companion.

"Ozzie?" said his mother. "How could you do such a thing?"

"You didn't say I couldn't," Ozzie pointed out. "And I thought it would cheer Dad up to see her."

"Your father is very, very sick," said his mother.

"You mean I can't see him?" asked Ozzie. "I'll leave Snow White outside. I could put her in the car," he offered.

Mrs. Sims put her arms around her son.

"Things are not good." She chose her words carefully. "Dad had a bad allergic reaction to the streptokinase—that's the medicine the doctor gave him for breaking blood clots. The medicine has made him worse. So you can't see him now after all."

"How can medicine make you worse? It's supposed to make you better," Ozzie said angrily.

"Sometimes it happens," said Nurse Millsap.

Ozzie stood looking down at Snow White in his hands and blinking away his tears. How could the nurse scold him and say that his mouse was going to bring germs into the hospital and at the same time the hospital was giving out medicines that made people sick instead of better?

"Come," said his mother, taking Ozzie by the arm and walking toward the exit.

"Where are we going?" Ozzie asked.

"I'm taking you and Snow White home. I've called Mrs. Menzer. She's going to stay with you this evening while I come and watch after Dad. He always said he married me so he could have his own private-duty nurse." Ozzie knew his mother was trying to make a joke, but her voice cracked in the middle and Ozzie thought she might start crying.

"Dad's very bad, isn't he?" he asked as they were driving home.

Mrs. Sims nodded her head and kept her eyes on the road.

"Shouldn't we let Joan and Steve and Roz know now?" Ozzie demanded. This bad news was too much to keep bottled up inside himself. He needed to share it with others who loved his father.

"No, no," Ozzie's mother said. "Other people have had allergic reactions and have made beautiful recoveries. Your father is getting the best medical care possible. And there's no sense in making them crazy with worry and spoiling their wonderful time in London."

Ozzie looked down at Snow White, who was wriggling about in his hands. He was sure the mouse agreed with him. His mother was making a bad decision. He wondered what he could do about it.

8
Ozzie Makes
a Phone Call

Ozzie felt awful. If only he could have seen his father at the hospital! He knew that taking Snow White along with him had had nothing to do with his father's turn for the worse. But somehow he felt as if he was responsible. Nurse Millsap had said that his mouse brought germs into the hospital.

There were leftovers for supper, but Ozzie wasn't very hungry.

"Is that all you're going to eat?" asked Mrs. Menzer, looking at the dishful of food. She had come to stay with Ozzie while his mother was at the hospital. "You're a growing boy! You didn't eat enough to fill a mouse."

"I'm full," said Ozzie, pushing the food around on his plate.

"I'll cover it with some plastic wrap. Maybe you'll want it later," suggested his neighbor.

Ozzie nodded his head, although he was certain he would never eat again—or at least not unless his father was well and home from the hospital. He put his plate of supper into the refrigerator. Seeing a bowl of blueberries, he took two. He would give them to Snow White as a treat. Unlike Ozzie, the white mouse had a great appetite and nibbled happily on whatever she was offered.

"I'm going to watch TV," Mrs. Menzer told Ozzie. "Why don't you keep me company?"

"I'll be back," said Ozzie. "I'm going to feed my mouse."

He went upstairs to his room. After stroking Snow White for a minute, Ozzie put the berries in her box. He'd have to figure out a better home for her, he realized. Then he went back downstairs and sat on the sofa next to Mrs. Menzer.

"I love to watch quiz shows," she told Ozzie. "My husband was very smart and knew more answers than any of these contestants. We could have gotten very rich if he'd ever gone on one of these shows."

Ozzie nodded his head and pretended he was listening. He really wanted to ask Mrs. Menzer about her husband's heart attack. Had he died right away? Maybe he had lived a few more years before he died.

Suddenly, Ozzie remembered something very important about his parents. It was something he rarely thought about because it had never seemed to concern him. Both his mother and his father had been married to other people a long time ago. Those other people had both died. Ozzie's half sister, Joan, who was Roz's mother, had lost her father when she was just about the same age that Ozzie was now. He had never talked to her about it. But now that he thought of it, he bet she had been very sad. He bet she felt just the way he felt now. And he bet she still remembered her father and missed him all these years later. It was just as likely that his father still thought about his other wife, the one he had before he married Ozzie's mother.

So many sad thoughts about dead people made Ozzie feel miserable. Mrs. Menzer was engrossed in her program, so she hardly noticed that Ozzie jumped up and ran up the stairs.

In his bedroom, Ozzie didn't have to hide his tears. He lay down on his bed and cried into his pillow. Even the sound of Snow White scratching away inside her box didn't comfort him. He felt totally alone in the world. Both his parents were at the hospital and his sister and her family were hundreds and hundreds of miles away. They didn't even guess that anything was wrong.

Ozzie sat up and blew his nose. If his father was dying, then Joan and Steve and Roz should know about it. They should know about it now, not after it happened. Somewhere he had once heard an expression: No news is good news. Well, that wasn't true at all. No news just meant that they hadn't been told. And that wasn't good. It wasn't right, either, he told himself.

Ozzie remembered what his mother had said to him. She had forbidden him to *write* to Roz and her parents about his father's heart attack. But it occurred to him that there was a way he could get around this without actually disobeying her. He could call them on the telephone and *talk* to them.

Ozzie blew his nose again. That's what he would do, he decided. He would phone his relatives in England and tell them the news. His mother hadn't forbidden him to do that.

Ozzie looked at the clock. It was just after eight o'clock. There was a five-hour time difference between here and England. He counted back, seven, six, five, four, three. If he was lucky, he'd find someone in right now. He hoped they weren't off sight-seeing again.

Ozzie decided to use the telephone in his parents' bedroom. That way, Mrs. Menzer wouldn't know what he was doing and she wouldn't try to stop him. She might feel just the way his mother did, that bad news shouldn't be shared. Unfortunately, the phone number of the apartment Roz and her parents were staying in was down in the kitchen.

Ozzie took off his shoes and tiptoed down the stairs. The television was loud enough to cover any sound he might make. He peeked into the living room. Mrs. Menzer's head was drooping down onto her chest. She had fallen asleep watching her program.

On the refrigerator was a magnet holding the information that Ozzie needed. He took the paper with the address and phone number in London. It was amazing to think that by pushing a few buttons on the telephone he was actually going to be able to talk to Roz or her parents when they were so very far away. They had phoned home once, just after they had arrived in England. But Ozzie hadn't been in the house when they called, so he had missed the chance to speak to them.

Ozzie was so nervous about what he was doing that he kept making errors and had to start over again. Finally, on the third try, he succeeded in pushing the correct sequence of numbers. He waited as the telephone rang on the other side of the ocean. The sound of the ringing phone was different from usual. There was a double ring instead of a single one.

Two rings and then a pause. Two rings and then a pause. Two rings and then a pause. There was no answer. Ozzie felt a sob welling up within his chest. He wanted to talk with his family so much and they weren't there. Two more rings and then he heard someone picking up the phone.

"Hello?" a man's voice answered.

"Hello?" Ozzie responded. He didn't recognize the voice. He was afraid that after all this he had gotten a wrong number.

"Who is it?" the voice asked. It seemed a little bit more familiar than it had a moment before.

"Steve? Is that you?" Ozzie asked hopefully.

"Ozzie? For goodness' sakes. What's the matter?"

"How do you know something's the matter?" Ozzie asked. He was amazed how clearly he could hear his brother-in-law. It was just as if he was talking from the next town and not from so far away.

"It's after midnight. It's one o'clock in the morning," the voice on the other end said.

"Oh," gasped Ozzie. "I counted the wrong way."

"Well, hello anyhow," said Steve. "How are things going?"

"Terrible," said Ozzie. He couldn't help himself. He began to cry again. It was so comforting to hear the familiar voice and such a relief to admit to someone how bad the situation was. "I'm all alone."

"Just because Roz is away for the summer doesn't mean you're all alone," said Steve. Ozzie knew Steve was remembering how much he had complained when Roz was getting ready to leave for their trip.

"Put your mother on. Let me say hello to her," said Steve.

"She's not here," said Ozzie. "She's at the hospital."

"Is she working? Then put your father on the line."

"My dad is at the hospital, too." Ozzie swallowed hard. Then he made the awful announcement. "He's sick. He had a heart attack last night. My mom didn't want me to tell you. But I just had

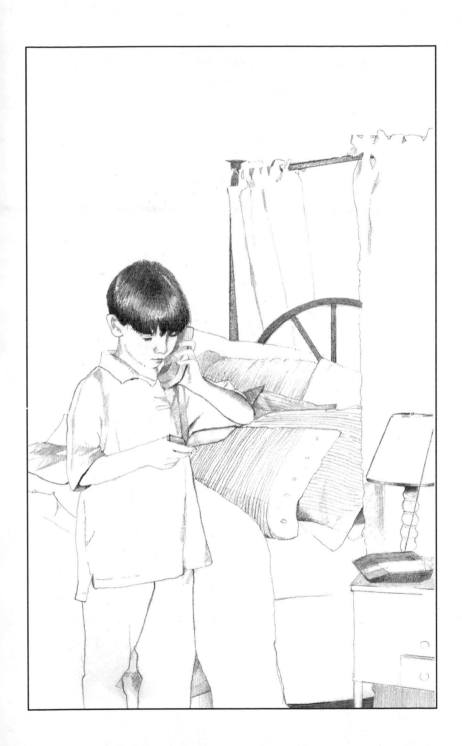

to." Ozzie wiped his nose with his shirt. Then he reached for a handful of tissues from the box near the phone.

"Who is it?" he heard a woman's voice asking Steve. It was Joan.

Ozzie tried to imagine them standing or sitting around the telephone in the middle of the night on the other side of the world. He could hear Steve telling Joan about her stepfather. He wondered if Roz was awake now, too.

"Ozzie, you did a good thing calling us," said Steve. Ozzie nodded his head even though his brother-in-law couldn't see him.

"I would have been very upset if we didn't know about this," Steve said.

"You don't have to come home," Ozzie pointed out. "I just thought I should tell you. That's all."

"I understand," said Steve. "Listen, kid. Don't despair. Your father is in a great hospital. He's got his own private nurse. He'll probably be home in a few days and be just fine."

"I know," said Ozzie, but he didn't believe it.

"It's almost bedtime in America, too," Steve said. "Try and get a good night's sleep. Your mother needs you to be strong and well. You're the man of the family while I'm away and your father is ill."

"Yes," said Ozzie, wiping his eyes with his hands and feeling anything but strong.

"Ozzie?" It was Joan's voice. "How is Dad?" she asked. Usually she called Ozzie's father George, which was his first name.

"I don't know," said Ozzie. "I don't think he's good. Mom's staying with him at the hospital."

"Thanks for calling us," Joan said. "It's important that we know what's going on."

"That's what I thought, too," said Ozzie, wiping the tears that were still running down his face.

"We'll keep in touch," said Joan. "And Ozzie," she added, "don't forget we love you. We'll always be here for you."

"Yes," whispered Ozzie.

"Good night," said Joan. And then the line went dead.

Ozzie reached for another tissue and blew his nose. He bent to pick up all the wet and rumpled tissues that he had thrown on the floor and he saw a pair of his father's shoes. They were the shoes he had taken off before he went to bed the night before. Ozzie stuck his bare feet inside the shoes. It was a game he had loved to play when he was little.

Even though Ozzie had grown, his father's

shoes were still many sizes too large. Ozzie's feet shuffled around the floor in the big shoes. When he was little, he had worn the shoes, pretending he was his father. Now he wore the shoes because they seemed to link him to his father despite the distance that separated them tonight.

Ozzie looked down at his feet. He felt awful. He wondered if his father would ever wear these shoes again.

9
Snow White
Stays Home

Ozzie decided that Mrs. Richards was a nice lady even though she had made Ryan get rid of Snow White. As soon as she learned from her children about Ozzie's father, Mrs. Richards had contacted Mrs. Sims. She offered to look after Ozzie while his mother was so busy running back and forth to the hospital.

It was arranged that on Friday, instead of spending their time in their clubhouse, Ozzie would go with Ryan and Ditto and their mother to the beach. Candy came along, too. So except for their mascots, Samantha and Snow White, it was a real Chicken Coop Club outing. If it wasn't for the awful fact that his father was still in intensive care at the hospital, Ozzie would have said it was one of the best days of his life.

The four friends splashed together in the ocean. It pleased Ozzie that this was the same ocean that touched the shores of England, where Roz was. Ozzie hoped that Roz was at the beach right now, too. Then they would both be in the same water at the same time. After eating a picnic lunch, Ozzie, Ryan, Ditto, and Candy built not just one castle in the sand but a whole town of castles. Before leaving the beach area, Mrs. Richards let the children go on some rides at the amusement park that was nearby.

It had been a busy, happy day for Ozzie because most of the time he forgot to worry about his father. But every once in a while the thought would suddenly come back. Here he was laughing and having fun and his father was in the hospital. Then Ozzie would stop laughing and become serious again.

"I think you got a hundred or so new freckles today," Mrs. Sims observed when Ozzie came home. "I wouldn't have thought that was possible."

Mrs. Sims was going to take Ozzie to the hospital that evening. "But no mice," she warned her son.

"I couldn't take *mice*," said Ozzie. "I only have *one* mouse."

"Well, don't take anything or do anything you shouldn't," she said. "I had to get special permission for you to go. And Dad is doing better. But we don't want him to have a relapse just because of something foolish that you do."

"I'll be good," Ozzie promised his mother. He was more anxious than ever to see his dad finally. He had never been separated from him for so long before.

It was a relief to Ozzie that there was no sign of Nurse Millsap when they arrived at the hospital. She probably wouldn't trust him after the other day. Instead, there was another woman, named Nurse Staples, who greeted Mrs. Sims and Ozzie.

"How is he?" asked Ozzie's mother anxiously, even though she had been at the hospital just a couple of hours before.

"He's coming along just fine," said Nurse Staples in a reassuring voice. "You can both go right in."

Ozzie took a deep breath. He wasn't quite sure what he would see. But happily, it wasn't as bad as he feared. His father was lying in bed with a tube coming out of his arm that hooked up to a bottle of some sort of clear liquid. Ozzie was relieved to see that he was awake. Although pale, Mr. Sims smiled when he saw his family.

"Look who came to see you," Nurse Staples said to Mr. Sims. "If I had a dime for each of your son's freckles, I'd be rich enough to retire."

"Ah yes," said Ozzie's father in a voice that was a little scratchy. "But if you had Ozzie for a son, you'd be better than rich. He makes me the happiest man alive. And that's something that money can't buy."

Ozzie wanted to give his father a hug, but the tube deterred him. It would be just his luck to knock it out accidentally or something. So instead, he just came up close to the bed and touched his father's arm gently. There was a plastic band on his father's wrist with his name on it: *George Sims*.

Mr. Sims reached for his son's hand and gave it a firm squeeze. "How're you doing?" he asked Ozzie. "I'm sorry I gave you and your mother such a big scare."

"That's okay," said Ozzie. Of course it wasn't okay, but he wasn't sure what else he should say. "I'm sorry I got so angry when you wouldn't come and see my clubhouse," he apologized to his father.

"You look one hundred percent better than you

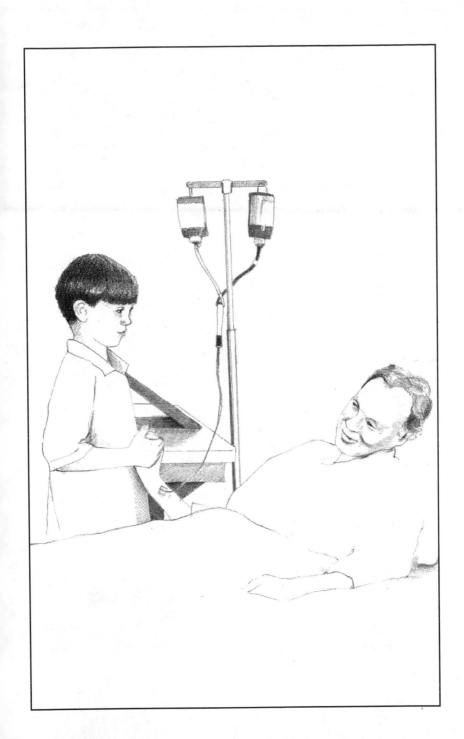

did this morning," Ozzie's mother told her husband.

"Now that you're here, I'm two hundred percent better," he replied.

Ozzie sat down on the edge of his father's bed. Even though there was a sheet separating them, it was comforting to feel the pressure of his father's leg. It made up for the unfamiliar hospital smell about the room and his father. There was a white stubble on his father's cheeks because he hadn't shaved. It made him look a lot older than he had two days ago.

Nurse Staples left the room. "I want to speak to the doctor if he's in," said Mrs. Sims. "I'll be right back. Can you take care of your father?" she asked Ozzie.

Although Ozzie realized there was nothing much that he could do, he knew his mother had just said it as a joke. He wasn't a doctor or a nurse. He was just a kid, and that left him pretty helpless in a situation like this.

"I hear you tried to bring a mouse to visit me," said Mr. Sims, smiling at his son.

Ozzie nodded. "Snow White," he said. "Mom wouldn't let me bring her this time. One of the nurses said that mice carry germs. But Snow White is clean and beautiful."

"I'll see her pretty soon. When I get home," said Ozzie's father.

"Will you have an operation?" Ozzie asked anxiously.

"The doctor says that it's possible I can correct my heart problems by watching my diet and getting more exercise. So we'll have to play ball more and take walks together. All right?"

Ozzie nodded his head, relieved by this news. "Do you hurt?" he asked his father.

"Not now. I did the other evening when I had the heart attack. Now I just feel weak. But hopefully that will go away soon," said Mr. Sims.

"Dad," said Ozzie, "can I ask you something?"

"Sure," said his father. "Is it a chicken riddle?"

"No," said Ozzie, blinking his eyes to prevent himself from crying. "This is serious. It isn't a joke or a riddle."

"I'll answer if I can," said Mr. Sims. "At home when you ask me hard questions, I can run to the encyclopedia if I don't know the answer. Here I don't have much help." He turned and pointed to two books with shiny covers that were resting on the little cabinet beside his bed. He had received them as gifts. There was also a magazine and a newspaper.

"Dad," said Ozzie. His mouth felt dry and he could hardly get the words out. But it was very important that he find out the answer. "Are you going to die?"

For a moment, Mr. Sims didn't respond. Then he took Ozzie's hand again before he spoke. "Of course I'm going to die," he said.

"You are?" Ozzie asked, startled. He had been afraid of his question and at the same time certain that his father would reassure him that everything was fine. This wasn't the answer he had expected to get.

"Everyone dies," said Mr. Sims. "But when I'm going to die is a riddle. It's the biggest riddle in the world. And it's not one that people joke about. Usually they sit around worrying about it instead. But you know what? You can't waste your time worrying. I hardly ever think about it, and you shouldn't, either."

"But Dad, you're so old. All the other kids have fathers who are lots younger. And now you're sick. Does that mean you'll die soon?"

"Ozzie, one of the things you learn when you

get older is that you don't go through life standing on line waiting your turn to die. Just because I'm older doesn't mean a thing. Every day people die who are much, much younger than I am. Sometimes they get incurable illnesses. Other times they are in accidents. When young people die, it isn't fair. But that's just the way life is."

Mr. Sims reached for the newspaper on the cabinet. "Here. Let's take a look at who died today."

He put on his reading glasses and began turning the pages of the paper until he found what he was searching for. "Look at this," he said, pointing to a picture of a man. "Herman J. Overbrook, age eighty-seven. That's not a bad age to live to. I'd have another thirty-one years to go."

Ozzie smiled. Thirty years seemed a century off. In thirty-one years, he'd be going on forty. He guessed he could take care of himself when he was forty years old.

"But look at this. James Roger Cooper, age twenty-three. You see what I mean? People die at all ages. And life goes on."

Ozzie thought about the unknown woman who had been his father's first wife. He thought about Joan's father, who had been his mother's first husband. If life hadn't gone on, he wouldn't be sitting here at this very moment, he realized.

"Ozzie, you can only live your life one day at a time. So it's better not to spend it all worrying about tomorrow—especially if worry about tomorrow means that you can't enjoy today. Today I am alive. I am with my son and I am trying to think of a good riddle to stump him before he has to go home. Then tomorrow, when it comes, I'll worry about that day and its problems."

Then Mr. Sims changed the subject. "Your mother tells me you've been busy making new friends this summer. That's great. You've always been a resourceful kid, able to have a good time on your own. But it's important to have friends, too."

"We have a super club," said Ozzie. "It's the Chicken Coop Club and I'm the president. We're going to make up new chicken riddles and jokes."

"Great!" said Mr. Sims. "You can probably help cure me right now by asking me a good riddle. They say that laughter is as good as any medicine. And I never heard of anyone having an allergic reaction to a good joke. So what do you have to cure me with today?"

Ozzie thought for a minute. He'd been so busy worrying that he had not made up any new riddles since his father's heart attack. Then he remembered the last one he'd written on his notepad.

"Do you know the difference between a chicken and an elephant?" he asked his father.

Mr. Sims thought for a moment. "You've got me there," he said to his son.

"Then you'll never get a job at the zoo," Ozzie told him.

Ozzie's father was laughing at his son's riddle and Ozzie was laughing with delight at his response when Mrs. Sims returned to the room.

10
Ketchup

The following evening, Ozzie sat at the table in his kitchen. He had a bowl, a bottle, and a box in front of him. The bottle was full of ketchup and the box contained pennies from his collection.

Ozzie was going to clean all his pennies using Mrs. Menzer's special ketchup method. He had read all the ingredients listed on the ketchup bottle aloud to his mother a few minutes ago: tomato paste, distilled vinegar, corn syrup, salt, onion powder, spice, natural flavoring. "What do you think makes it work like magic to clean a penny?" he had asked his mother.

"I guess it's the acid in the vinegar," she had said. "But I must confess that I would never have thought to suggest it to you in a thousand years."

Now, instead of just putting a little ketchup between his fingers the way Mrs. Menzer had shown him, Ozzie poured a generous amount of the sauce into the bowl. Then he dumped his pennies in the bowl, too. He put his hands in the bowl and picked out a single coin at a time to be rubbed.

As he worked, his mother was standing nearby and speaking on the phone. The phone had seemed to ring a lot in the last couple of days as various friends and acquaintances somehow learned the news about Ozzie's father. Everyone had called to find out how he was doing.

Ozzie looked up from his bowl of pennies and ketchup and glanced at his mother. She still didn't know that he had called Joan and Steve in England.

Just as his mother was hanging up the phone, there was a sound from the side door. Someone was opening the door. Ozzie's face lighted up with a fantastic thought. Could it be that his father had been released from the hospital and had come home?

"Who's there?" called Mrs. Sims in an anxious tone. Except for Ozzie's father and Joan and Steve off in England, no one else had a key for that side door.

To the amazement of both Ozzie and his mother, there was Steve coming through the little entryway.

"Steve, what are you doing here? Is something wrong?" Mrs. Sims called out in a startled voice.

"Steve! Steve!" Ozzie shouted, jumping up and knocking his chair onto the floor in his excitement. He threw his arms around his brother-in-law.

"What happened to your hands?" asked Steve with alarm.

"Nothing," said Ozzie.

"Nothing? You're bleeding!" said Steve.

"No I'm not," said Ozzie, laughing at Steve's mistake. "It's only ketchup."

Ozzie held his hands up to Steve's nose so he could smell the familiar odor of ketchup. He noticed with guilt that he had gotten ketchup on Steve's shirt when he had hugged him.

"Steve," said Mrs. Sims again, "what are you doing here?"

"I live here," Steve reminded his mother-in-law. "But the real reason I'm here is to check up on George's health. Ozzie told me about his heart attack."

"Ozzie?" said Mrs. Sims in amazement. "How could he do that? You were in England."

"You'll see how he could do it when you get your phone bill," said Steve, laughing.

Mrs. Sims turned to Ozzie. "When did you do that?" she asked.

"I phoned a couple of nights ago. You told me not to write and say anything. But you never said anything about phoning. And I just felt that Steve and Joan and Roz should know about Dad. I had to tell them even if you didn't want me to."

"Of course he had to tell us. You could have told us yourself," Steve said to his mother-in-law. "What is family for if we aren't there to support and console one another in bad times as well as good?"

Mrs. Sims grabbed a tissue from a box on the kitchen counter and wiped her eyes. "I didn't want Joan to worry. This was such a great opportunity for her, a chance to do her studies and to do some traveling—and for you and Roz to have a good time, too."

Ozzie's mother blew her nose and went to embrace Steve. As she approached him, she noticed something. "Steve, you've hurt yourself. You're bleeding," she said with concern.

"It's just ketchup," shouted Ozzie. He had always heard that bleeding people in movies had ketchup coming out of their fake wounds. He had never believed it. Now he did.

"What kind of nurse are you anyhow?" Steve asked his mother-in-law as he gave her a hug. "You can't even tell the difference between blood and ketchup."

The three of them laughed at that.

"Where're Roz and Joan?" asked Ozzie.

"They're still in England. But I came to check on your father."

"He's improving every day," Mrs. Sims reassured Steve.

"We tried phoning several times after Ozzie called us," Steve said. "But what with the time difference and you people going to the hospital, we never found anyone in. And when we phoned the hospital, they wouldn't give us very much information. So in the end, Joan and I decided that I should come back home. And I went directly to the hospital even before I came here. Even though it wasn't visiting hours, they let me see George for a few minutes. I think they were impressed when I waved my airplane ticket at them." Steve smiled at Ozzie and his mother. "George is going to be fine," he said.

"Yes, he is," agreed Mrs. Sims, smiling happily.

"It's good to have you here, Steve," she added.

"So you aren't angry at me?" asked Ozzie.

"No," said his mother. "I should have remembered that you never do things I tell you not to do but that you often do things it never occurs to me to mention. I never said a word about telephoning."

"Ozzie, you did absolutely the right thing. Thank you very much for calling," said Steve. He sat down at the kitchen table, next to the bowl of ketchup.

"What in the world are you cooking?" he asked.

"I'm not cooking. I'm cleaning. This is Mrs. Menzer's magic way to clean old coins. Look." Ozzie held out a shiny penny for his brother-in-law to admire.

"Nice trick," Steve agreed. "But wash your hands. I have a present for you."

Ozzie rushed to the sink to rinse the ketchup from his fingers.

"Here," said Steve, pulling a small box out of the zippered luggage case he had with him.

Ozzie opened the box eagerly. Inside was a very fancy-looking wristwatch.

"I'm going to stay around for a bit to see how things are going here," said Steve. "But if you decide to phone Roz or Joan, I want you to be able to figure out the correct time. No more calling in the middle of the night."

"Wow. This watch has everything," said Ozzie. The new watch not only told the time—hours and minutes and seconds—but it gave the full date, including the day of the week and the month. It had an alarm and could be used as a stopwatch. Around the face of the watch was a compass. Ozzie took out the instruction sheet that was in the box and started reading it. "Wow," he said again. "This watch is water-resistant to a depth of one hundred feet."

"Maybe so," said Steve. "But don't drop it down the toilet to test it."

"Oh, Steve," said Ozzie, giving his brother-in-law another hug. "It's so great to have you home. I missed you all so much. I was so scared and I felt so alone."

"Listen," said Steve. "The real reason I came home was to see you as much as your parents. I want you to know that you'll never be alone. Don't you ever forget that we are all your family."

Hearing Steve's words, Ozzie felt like crying. He bent his head to look at his watch more closely so his brother-in-law wouldn't notice.

"Let me help you put it on," offered Steve. "But don't get ketchup on it. The instructions don't say if it's ketchup-proof."

"You must be starving," said Ozzie's mother. "I'll fix you something to eat."

So while Mrs. Sims started preparing a small meal for Steve, Ozzie put his bowl of ketchup, with the pennies still in it, inside the refrigerator for another day.

"Oh, here," said Steve, putting his hand into his pocket and then giving Ozzie a coin. "I found this penny in the airport. Maybe you can use it for your collection."

The coin was shiny enough that Ozzie didn't have to treat it with ketchup in order to read the date. "Hey, this penny was minted the year I was born," said Ozzie delightedly. "That's good luck."

"You don't need pennies for luck," said Steve. "You make your own luck."

"I know," said Ozzie, smiling at his brother-in-law. He knew he was lucky to have Steve and Joan and Roz, even if Joan and Roz were so far away. He was lucky to have his parents, too, even if his father was still in the hospital. He was lucky to have his clubhouse and his new friends, Ryan and Ditto and Candy. He didn't have to worry about being on his own. There were loads of people in his life. Mrs. Menzer, too, he realized. And Snow White—even if she was a mouse and not a person.

"Ozzie, you haven't been doing any coin-cleaning magic with the mayonnaise, have you?" called Mrs. Sims. "I can't seem to find the jar." Her head was inside the refrigerator as she spoke.

"Oh, no," said Ozzie. "That new jar I bought should be in there someplace." He squeezed in next to his mother and reached onto the bottom shelf of the refrigerator. Triumphantly, he retrieved the mayonnaise.

Then he went and sat down next to Steve. For the first time in days he was feeling really hungry, too. "You don't want to eat alone, do you?" he asked his brother-in-law.

DATE DUE			
11805			
1/31/06			

F
HUR

Hurwitz, Johanna.

Ozzie on his own

MYRON J.FRANCIS SCHOOL LIBRARY
RUMFORD, RI 02916
PTA Funding

569773 01275 51259B 02616E